For Jo – NL
For Daniel – TW

Copyright © 2010 by Good Books, Intercourse, PA 17534
International Standard Book Number: 978-1-56148-681-6

Library of Congress Catalog Card Number 2009031143

Text copyright © Norbert Landa 2010
Illustrations copyright © Tim Warnes 2010
Original edition published in English by Little Tiger Press,
an imprint of Magi Publications, London, England, 2010
Printed in Singapore
Library of Congress Cataloging-in-Publication Data

Landa, Norbert.

The great monster hunt / Norbert Landa;
[illustrations] Tim Warnes.

p. cm.

Summary: When Duck hears a noise under
her bed and runs to fetch help, each animal
that hears about it imagines a more
dangerous beast in Duck's room.

ISBN 978-1-56148-681-6
(hardcover : alk. paper)
[1. Imagination--Fiction.
2. Fear--Fiction.
3. Animals--Fiction.]
I. Warnes, Tim, ill. II. Title.

PZ7.L23165Gr 2010

[E]--dc22

2009031143

The Great Monster Hunt

Norbert Landa

Tim Warnes

Good Books

Intercourse, PA 17534, 800/762-7171, www.GoodBooks.com

Early one morning, a funny noise woke up Duck.
It sounded like, ρShh ρShh! and it came from
right under her bed.

Duck was not quite sure what it was,
and she was much too afraid to look.

Pshh pShh!

Instead, she jumped out of bed
and ran for help.

"Pig!" Duck yelled. "There is something under my bed and it's making strange sounds. It goes, pshh pshh, **grrr**!"

"Pshh pshh, **grrr**?" asked Pig.
"Oh my! We need someone really strong to help. Stay right where you are!"

And Pig ran to find Bear.

Pig told Bear all about the frightening noise under Duck's bed. "It goes,

pshh pshh,

grrr,

bang bang!

I wanted to tell you, Bear, because you are so strong."

Bear lifted a huge log. "It is true I am strong enough for almost anything," he said. "But I think we'd better find someone who is *loud* enough to chase this thing away."

Bear told him the dreadful news about the terrifying thing under Duck's bed.

So they ran to find Wolf, who was about to start his early morning howling.

"It goes, pshh pshh, grrr, bang bang, wham wham –

all of the time!" Bear said.

"We thought you could help us frighten it away!"

"Oh yes, I can!" Wolf proudly said.

"There is no match for what I can do. Just listen!

OWO OOOOOOO!

But maybe we also need help from someone really clever."

So they ran to find Owl.

"Listen," Wolf said. "There is a dreadful and terrifying sound under Duck's bed. It goes, pshh pshh, **grrr,**

bang bang, wham wham, grrrrowl!"

Owl was lost for words.

"We thought you might know what it was," Pig said, "because you are so clever."

Owl said, "Clever, yes, that's what I am.
So I can tell you one thing:

Duck is in great danger!"

Pig, Bear and Wolf huddled closer together.
"Are you sure?" they asked.

"Oh yes," Owl said. "Can you imagine anything
kind and cuddly making such a noise?"

"It must be a monster!" yelled Pig.
"Oh, what are we going to do?"

"The only way to deal with
a monster," Owl said, "is to trap it."

Clever Owl!

So the animals set about gathering rope and nets and useful pokey things. Then the four of them bravely set off toward Duck's house.

Owl led the way, because trapping the monster was his clever idea. Next came Wolf, howling loudly. Then came Bear, with his monster-buster stick. Last was Pig, clutching his great monster-catcher net.

Finally they arrived at Duck's house
and flattened their ears against the door.
But no monstrous sound was heard—no
screaming nor crying nor calling for help.
   "Maybe we are too late?" whispered Bear.
   "Oh nooo!" Pig cried in despair.
   "Duck, are you there?" called Wolf.

Then the door slowly creaked open . . .

It was Duck. "You're here!" she said.

"Duck! You are in great danger!"
whispered Bear.

"There's a monster
under your bed!" cried Pig.

Duck looked ready to faint.

"A monster?" she whimpered.

"How do you know?"

It was Duck. "You're here!" she said.
"Duck! You are in great danger!"
whispered Bear.

"There's a monster
under your bed!" cried Pig.

Duck looked ready to faint.
"A monster?" she whimpered.
"How do you know?"

Then the door slowly creaked open . . .

"Because it goes,

pshh pshh, grrr,
bang bang,
wham wham,
grrrrowl!" Pig yelled.

"And,

OOOOOOOOOeeeee!"

Owl added.

"Come on, let's get it!"
And the animals charged
into Duck's house.

Up the stairs they crept . . . then they heard a sound.

PShh pShh! it went.

It came from right under Duck's bed.

Owl flashed his lantern. The animals gasped.

They could not believe their eyes!

pshh pshh!

There, right under Duck's bed, was a tiny mouse,
snoring softly in its tiny bed, pShh pShh!
"Well I never!" Duck whispered.
"Do you know what we've just done?" Owl smiled.
All feeling rather silly, the animals looked at each
other and giggled . . .

"We've just made a **monster** out of a mouse!"